D1098813

Leabharlainn nan Eilean Siar

RESOURCE CENTRE
WESTERN ISLES LIBRARIES

PRIMARY 1-3

NURSERY

Readers are requested to take great care of the item while in their possession, and to point out any defects that they may notice in them to the Librarian.
This item should be returned on or before the latest date stamped below, but an extention of the period of loan may be granted when desired.

DATE OF RETURN	DATE OF RETURN	DATE OF RETURN
L.O.T. ... 22		
L.O.T. ... 1.7.		
P1-3 ... Box 17		
" ... Box 3		

LIBRARY STOCK

WITHDRAWN

First published 2005
Evans Brothers Limited
2A Portman Mansions
Chiltern Street
London W1U 6NR

Text copyright © Evans Brothers Limited 2005
© in the illustrations Evans Brothers Limited 2005

All rights reserved. No part of this publication
may be reproduced, stored in a retrieval system
or transmitted in any form, or by any means,
electronic, mechanical, photocopying, recording
or otherwise, without the prior permission of
Evans Brothers Limited.

British Library Cataloguing in Publication Data

Turpin, Nick
        Out went Sam. - (Twisters)
        1. Children's stories - Pictorial works
        I. Title
        823.9'2 [J]

ISBN 0 237 52894 0

Printed in China by WKT Company Limited

Series Editor: Nick Turpin
Design: Robert Walster
Production: Jenny Mulvanny
Series Consultant: Gill Matthews

Out Went Sam

Nick Turpin
and Barbara Nascimbeni

WESTERN ISLES
LIBRARIES
J30550149

Evans

Out went Sam.

Slam!

6

"Mind the door!" said Mum.

10

"Sorry!"

Splash went Sam.

12

13

"Mind the floor!"
said Mum.

"Sorry!"

16

18

Bounce went Sam.

"Mind the bed!" said Mum.

"Sorry!"

"Into the bath!" said Mum.

24

Squirt went Mum.

"Mind my eyes!"
said Sam.

"Sorry!" said Mum.

30

Why not try reading another Twisters book?

Not-so-silly Sausage by Stella Gurney and Liz Million
ISBN 0 237 52875 4
Nick's Birthday by Jane Oliver and Silvia Raga
ISBN 0 237 52896 7
Out Went Sam by Nick Turpin and Barbara Nascimbeni
ISBN 0 237 52894 0
Yummy Scrummy by Paul Harrison and Belinda Worsley
ISBN 0 237 52876 2
Squelch! by Kay Woodward and Stefania Colnaghi
ISBN 0 237 52895 9
Sally Sails the Seas by Stella Gurney and Belinda Worsley
ISBN 0 237 52893 2

If you liked Twisters try a ZigZag!

Dinosaur Planet by David Orme and Fabiano Fiorin
ISBN 0 237 52793 6
Tall Tilly by Jillian Powell and Tim Archbold
ISBN 0 237 52794 4
Batty Betty's Spells by Hilary Robinson and Belinda Worsley
ISBN 0 237 52795 2
The Thirsty Moose by David Orme and Mike Gordon
ISBN 0 237 52792 8
The Clumsy Cow by Julia Moffatt and Lisa Williams
ISBN 0 237 52790 1
Open Wide! by Julia Moffatt and Anni Axworthy
ISBN 0 237 52791 X
Too Small by Kay Woodward and Deborah van de Leijgraaf
ISBN 0 237 52777 4
I Wish I Was An Alien by Vivian French and Lisa Williams
ISBN 0 237 52776 6
The Disappearing Cheese by Paul Harrison and Ruth Rivers
ISBN 0 237 52775 8
Terry the Flying Turtle by Anna Wilson and Mike Gordon
ISBN 0 237 52774 X
Pet To School Day by Hilary Robinson and Tim Archbold
ISBN 0 237 52773 1
The Cat in the Coat by Vivian French and Alison Bartlett
ISBN 0 237 52772 3